Please return on or before the latest date above.
You can renew online at www.kent.gov.uk/libs
or by phone 08458 247 200

CUSTOMER SERVICE EXCELLENCE

Libraries & Archives

SCREAM STREET

BLOOD OF THE WITCH

TOMMY DONBAVAND

WALKER
BOOKS

This is a work of fiction. Names, characters, places and incidents are either the product of the author's imagination or, if real, are used fictitiously.

First published 2008 by Walker Books Ltd
87 Vauxhall Walk, London SE11 5HJ

2 4 6 8 10 9 7 5 3 1

Text © 2008 Tommy Donbavand
Illustrations © 2008 Cartoon Saloon Ltd

The right of Tommy Donbavand to be identified
as author of this work has been asserted by him in accordance
with the Copyright, Designs and Patents Act 1988

This book has been typeset in Bembo Educational

Printed and bound in Great Britain by Clays Ltd, St Ives plc

British Library Cataloguing in Publication Data: a catalogue record for this book is available from the British Library

ISBN 978-1-4063-1425-0

www.walker.co.uk

For Dad, who always knew it was in my blood

Meet the residents...

Luke Watson

Cleo Farr

Resus Negative

Dixon

Sir Otto Sneer

Samuel Skipstone

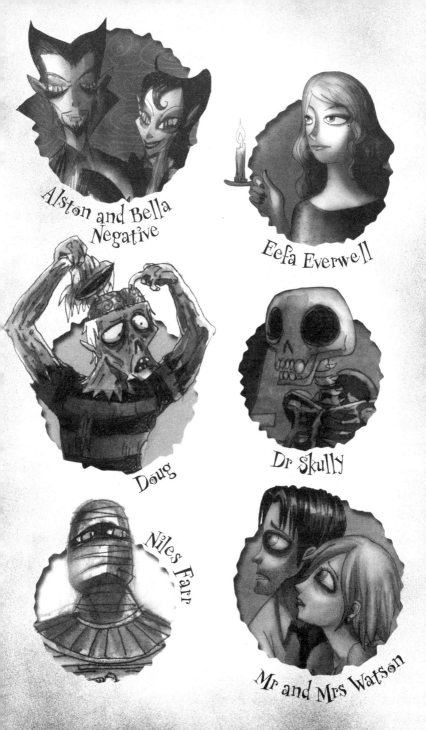

Alston and Bella
Negative

Eefa Everwell

Doug

Dr Skully

Niles Farr

Mr and Mrs Watson

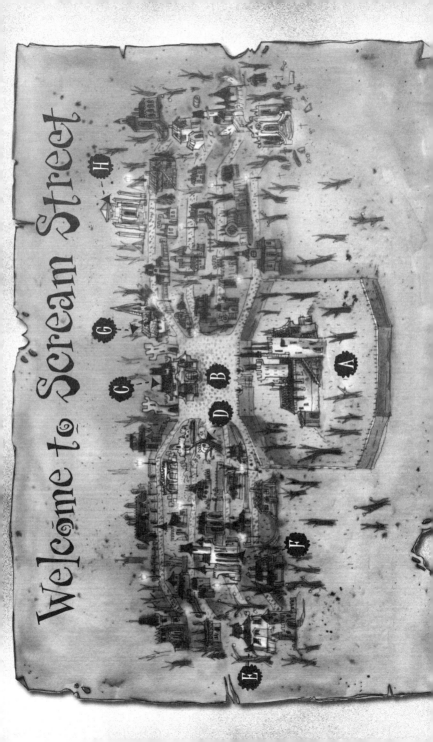

Who lives where...

A Sheer Hall

B Central square

C Everwell's Emporium

D No. 11: Twinkle

E No. 13: Luke Watson

F No. 14: Resus Negative

G No. 21: Eefa Everwell

H No. 22: Cleo Farr

Previously on Scream Street...

Luke Watson was a perfectly ordinary boy until his tenth birthday, when he transformed into a werewolf. After it happened twice more, Luke and his family were forcibly moved by G.H.O.U.L. (Government Housing Of Unusual Life-forms) to Scream Street, a community of ghosts, monsters, zombies and more.

Luke quickly found his feet, making friends with Cleo Farr (a tomboy mummy) and Resus Negative, the son of the vampires next door. Luke soon realized, however, that Mr and Mrs Watson would never get over their fear of their nightmarish neighbours. With the help of an ancient book, *Skipstone's Tales of Scream Street*, he set out to find six relics, each left behind by one of the community's founding fathers. Only their combined power will enable him to open a doorway out of Scream Street and take his parents home.

Luke, Resus and Cleo battled goblins and survived poltergeists to find the first relic: the fang of the ancient vampire, Count Negatov. Now, with Mr and Mrs Watson as terrified as ever, the quest is on to locate the second...

Chapter One
The Blood

Blood trickled down the vampire's fangs. A long tongue flicked out and licked the sticky fluid from sharp glistening teeth. The vampire's mouth twisted into a smile as it savoured the taste. It wanted more.

Lashing out, the vampire used its yellowing talons to tear another hunk of meat from the carcass. Pausing only to drench it in the nearby pool of blood, the creature bit into strips of flesh, veins

and tendons swinging below its salivating jaw. Suddenly a cry rang out.

"Dad! Leave some for everyone else!"

Alston Negative glanced around the dinner table and slowly placed the chicken wing back onto his plate. "Sorry," he mumbled, shamefaced.

Resus Negative, the vampire's son, reached inside his electric-blue-lined cape and produced a knife and fork. Handing them to his father, he added, "And you know you should be using cutlery when we have visitors."

As Alston fumbled with the unfamiliar tools, Resus nudged his friend, Luke Watson. "You don't make that much mess when you eat – and you're a werewolf!"

Luke grinned as he watched the older vampire push the chicken wing off his plate, catapulting potatoes across the black dining-room carpet.

"Being a vampire does have its advantages," joked Alston, leaping from his chair. "When I'm tired of biting necks, I double as a vegetable rack!" He pecked at the carpet and reappeared with a potato stuck to each fang.

"Dad," groaned Resus, embarrassed. "You're not funny!"

Luke roared with laughter and turned to his parents to share the joke. His face fell when he realized that the get-together hadn't worked. His mum and dad were still terrified of their vampire neighbours.

"A toast!" beamed Alston, pulling the potatoes from his teeth and raising a glass of wine. "To the Watsons, and your first week in Scream Street!"

"The Watsons!" echoed Resus, lifting his tumbler of milk. He clinked it against Luke's and drank deeply, his fangs tinkling against the rim of the glass. Instead of drinking his own milk, Luke reached out to take his mum's trembling hand and guide it towards her wine.

Mrs Watson forced a smile. "Thank you," she whispered hoarsely.

Luke and Resus shared a glance. Luke's family had been moved to Scream Street by G.H.O.U.L., Government Housing Of Unusual Life-forms, after he had transformed into his werewolf form and attacked a school bully. Since then his parents had lived in a state of sheer terror.

In order to open a doorway back to his own world, Luke had begun the search for six relics left behind by the community's founding fathers: their combined power was Luke's only hope for taking his family home The first relic, a vampire's fang, was now locked away in a golden casket under his bed.

"Now," said Bella Negative as she entered carrying a jug of thick red liquid, "who wants more blood on their meat?"

Mr Watson stared at the jug and paled. "I think I'm going to be sick…"

"I'll get you some water," said Luke, racing into the kitchen. Reaching for the cold tap, he stopped. The sink had three taps. "Resus!" he called.

The young vampire hurried in. "You summoned me?" he teased.

"Which one is cold water?" Luke asked.

"Isn't it obvious?" replied Resus. He gestured from left to right. "Hot water, cold water, blood."

"*Blood?*" exclaimed Luke. "You've got a *tap* for *blood*?"

"Of course," said Resus. "How else do you think vampires get their fix? We need a regular supply." He spun the tap, allowing a torrent of crimson blood to flow out into the sink. It spattered against the stainless steel, leaving behind small clots and scabs as it raced for the plughole.

"B–but a *tap*?" stammered Luke. "Where does it come from?"

"Whenever anyone has a nosebleed or a cut

finger and they rinse the blood away, it ends up in the sewer system," explained Resus. "The blood is filtered out and fed to vampires around the world."

"That's disgusting!"

"No more disgusting than how our ancestors used to get it." Resus opened his mouth and bared his fangs at Luke with a hiss.

Bella Negative appeared behind him. "Getting a drink of blood?" she asked, ruffling her son's hair.

"Luke knows I'm a normal like his mum and dad," Resus sighed. "He knows I'm not a real vampire!" He unclipped his false fangs and rinsed them briefly under the water before re-attaching them to his teeth. Suddenly the stream of blood stopped, the last remaining drips pattering against the sink.

"That's odd," said Resus. He opened the cupboard under the sink and reached past boxes of coffin polish and fang-whitener to check the stopcock.

Luke crouched down beside him. "Maybe there's a safety drive on and people have stopped grazing their knees," he grinned.

"I hope not," said Resus. "My dad gets really cranky without his daily pint!"

"Er, Luke," called Alston from the dining room, "I think your parents are ready to go home now."

Luke stood and turned to see his mum smiling bravely, his dad's arm tight around her shoulders. "I've got to take them away from here," he said quietly to Resus. "They're never going to be happy as long as we're in Scream Street."

"You mean…?" began the young vampire.

Luke nodded. "It's time to find the second relic."

The following morning, Luke was examining the fang of the ancient vampire Count Negatov when a bandaged hand snatched it from his fingers. "Hey!" he shouted.

"I just want a look," said the small Egyptian mummy. "I went through a lot to help you get that!" Cleo Farr was the third member of the relic-hunting team.

"Fresh air at last!" gasped a voice. With a smile, Luke reached inside the golden casket and retrieved *Skipstone's Tales of Scream Street*. The face of its author, Samuel Skipstone, gazed up from the book's silver cover.

"I appreciate the need for security," it announced, "but do you have to keep me in this infernal box? It stinks!"

"Well, it did contain my lungs for nearly six thousand years," said Cleo.

"Six thousand years?"

"They were removed before I was mummified," explained Cleo. "I expect anyone's insides would pong after that long!"

"I'm sorry, Mr Skipstone," apologized Luke, "but for the time being this is the best place for you."

"Yes," agreed Cleo. "You don't want to be found by Sir Otto again."

Skipstone scowled. "The sooner this street is released from the grip of that vile man, the better," he said. "If he were to find the relics of the founding fathers, he could make the lives of the residents a misery. You must keep me safe."

Cleo poked her tongue out at the book through her bandages. "So, what do you reckon to my smelly casket now?"

The author smiled. "I shall bear my troubles with fortitude!"

"It's only until we've found all the relics," said Luke.

"I understand," said Samuel Skipstone. "And I trust you have returned to ask the location of the gift of the second founding father?"

Luke nodded. "My mum and dad are unhappy. I have to take them home."

"Shouldn't we wait for Resus?" asked Cleo.

Luke checked his watch. Despite the stars flickering outside the window, it was actually only ten o'clock in the morning. The constant state of night that hung over Scream Street was playing havoc with his sense of time.

"He promised to be here first thing," said Luke. "I'm sure he won't mind if we start without him just once."

Skipstone's Tales of Scream Street opened itself and flipped through pages of handwritten articles, menus and experiments.

"Read carefully, my friends," said its author.

Luke and Cleo watched as the book stopped at an article detailing the various uses of bat's brains. Slowly the writing began to disappear, revealing hidden text beneath. They leant closer.

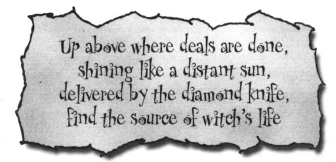

Up above where deals are done,
shining like a distant sun,
delivered by the diamond knife,
find the source of witch's life

"*Up above where deals are done,*" said Cleo. "I wonder where—"

Before she could get any further, the bedroom door crashed open and Resus ran in.

"Guys," he panted. "Something's happened to my dad!"

"What?" demanded Luke.

Resus tried to catch his breath. "He's gone missing!"

Chapter Two
The Sewers

"It can't be that bad," said Luke as he, Resus and Cleo hurried along Scream Street. "He's only been without blood since last night. Less than twenty-four hours."

"Trust me," said Resus, "my dad gets withdrawal symptoms. I swear he looked at my neck and licked his lips as I went to bed last night."

"Isn't it against vampire law to drink from your own family?" asked Cleo.

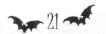

Resus nodded. "He's desperate, though. My mum said he went out just after midnight and didn't come back. We're hoping Everwell's Emporium will have something we can use to track him down. She's waiting at home in case he comes back."

"Isn't your mum affected too?" said Luke.

Resus shook his head. "She's been on a low-blood diet for years," he replied. "It'll take a lot longer for the effects to kick in with her."

Luke pushed open the shining silver doors to the general store that stood on Scream Street's central square. A bat perched above the door let out a shriek to announce the arrival of new customers. The emporium was empty.

"Where's Eefa?" asked Cleo.

"No idea," said Luke, "but I know where her latest batch of sweets is!" He snatched a sample of toffee from the counter and popped it into his mouth. "Mmm!"

"Look," said Resus. "The storeroom's open."

Cleo glanced up from the make-up display where she was busy applying a deep pink blusher to the bandages on her cheeks. "She must be in there."

Resus led the way through the back of the shop

and found, among the boxes, an open manhole in the middle of the storeroom. "Eefa!" he shouted.

"Down here!" came the reply. Luke, Resus and Cleo crowded around the hole in the floor and peered into the darkness.

"What are you doing in the sewer?" called Cleo.

A candle appeared below the hole. The flame flickered beside Eefa Everwell's flawless skin and glinted against her long white hair. As always, Luke was struck by how beautiful she was. He knew it was just an enchantment charm, but as he gazed at her he knew he would forgive Eefa anything.

"My blood supply has stopped," complained the witch. "I hoped I might find the problem down

here, but I can't see anything in this candlelight."

"I thought it was just vampires that had a blood supply," said Resus.

Eefa climbed back up through the manhole. "I use blood in all sorts of potions and recipes," she said. "It makes my home-made toffee nice and sticky, for one."

Cleo laughed as Luke spat out his half-chewed sweet, realizing there was something he wasn't prepared to forgive Eefa for after all.

"It's the perfect dye for my blusher, too," added Eefa.

Now it was Luke's turn to laugh as Cleo rubbed furiously at the spreading pink stains on her cheeks.

"Whatever the fault is, I can't find it," sighed the witch.

"Our supply's off too," said Resus. "But we'll take a look if you want."

Cleo went first, carefully avoiding the old tree roots that had pushed through the walls of the stone pipe. She held the ladder steady for Luke and Resus to join her in the darkness. "We need some light," she said.

"Voilà!" announced Resus, pulling a flaming wooden torch from his cape.

"I'm telling you," said Luke. "You could make a fortune selling those cloaks. Where I'm from, there's this thing called the Internet…"

Resus and Cleo didn't reply. Instead they stood frozen to the spot, staring at the thousands of pairs of eyes now reflecting the flickering torchlight. They were surrounded by rats.

"Ugh," shrieked Luke. "I hate these things. He swung a leg out towards the rats, shouting, "Go on, shoo!" The creatures didn't move.

"They're not so bad," said Cleo, crouching

down and extending her fingers towards them. "We used to have a family of rats in my tomb. So long as they don't consider you a threat, they'll leave you alo—"

She screamed. One of the rats had leapt forward and nipped her hand with its sharp teeth.

"I guess that one considers you a threat, then," grinned Resus.

"What did it do that for?" demanded Cleo, rubbing at her fingers.

"It's a rat," replied Luke. "It doesn't need an excuse to bite you."

"That's not it," said Resus, holding out the torch to scare the rat back to its pack. "Something's spooked them and they're defending their territory."

"Look!" hissed Cleo, pointing further down the sewer pipe. A figure moved in the shadows. Its pale face shone briefly in the torchlight, then it turned and ran.

"Who was *that*?" said Resus.

"And what are they doing down here in the dark?" added Luke.

"I don't know," said Cleo, "but it's possible they've got something to do with the blood supply being disconnected. Let's go after them!"

Luke gestured towards the swarm of rats still blocking their way. "Be my guest!"

As Cleo strode towards the rodents she was rewarded with another bite, this time on her toe. "There must be a way to get past!" she snapped.

Resus sighed. "Leave it to the vampire again." He reached inside his cloak and pulled out a large black cat.

"No way!" said Cleo.

"Why not?" asked Resus. "It's perfectly normal for me to have a metre-long piece of burning wood in my cloak, but when I pull out a cat, it's unusual?" With a grunt he hurled the cat among the pack of rats.

The effect was instant. Squealing, the rats scattered in every direction as they tried to avoid the hissing animal. The cat caught one of the slower rodents in its mouth, shaking the creature violently from side to side until it stopped wriggling.

Then, with a yowl, it raced into the darkness after the others.

Resus bowed to Luke and Cleo. "After you," he grinned.

The sewer pipe ended in an old rusted metal door, secured by a heavy latch.

Luke glanced down at a grille in the floor which was designed to carry waste water deeper underground. The concrete around the hole had broken away, and a clump of black fur clung to the ragged stone. "Unless whoever it was squeezed through that gap like the cat did, they went through this door."

"It doesn't look as though it's been opened for years," said Resus, running his hands over the rough surface. Rust crumbled away beneath his fingertips.

"Well, it must have been," said Luke. "And if we want to find out who else is down here with us, it'll have to open again now."

Lifting the latch, Luke, Resus and Cleo pressed their shoulders against the door and pushed. Slowly, it began to open. Once there was room to squeeze through, Luke slid a block of concrete up against the door to wedge it open.

The smell inside the room was dreadful. Cleo screwed up her nose. "What *is* that?" she asked.

Resus held up the torch to find out. Machinery

filled most of the room, with engines and control panels from floor to ceiling. Lying around the base of the machines were dozens of dead rats.

Resus took a step into the room. "Be careful you don't slip…" he began before the torch was knocked out of his hand. It clattered to the ground, the fire extinguishing with a hiss as it

landed in a mound of rodent droppings.

"Stay away!" screamed a voice.

"I'm warning you," shouted Resus, "we're armed! We've got a werewolf, and we're not afraid to use him!" The vampire's fingers touched something and he clutched tightly to an unseen arm. "Luke, I've got him!"

"You idiot!" bellowed Cleo. "That's me!"

"Sorry!"

Luke felt a figure brush past him and he grabbed what felt like a wrist in the darkness. "Got you!"

The figure lashed out. An elbow made contact with Luke's stomach and he crumpled to the floor, groaning as a familiar feeling began to wash over him.

"Luke?" said Cleo. "What's wrong?"

"I'm… I'm starting to change," gasped Luke.

"I can't find you," said Resus. "Keep talking! Cleo – find the torch."

Luke tried to speak but couldn't form any sounds. "I'm … here…" he mouthed. The words swam around his mind as his consciousness began to drift away. His skull stretched into a new, longer shape. Sharp fangs burst through his gums, pushing his own teeth aside as they fought to be free.

It was another of the partial transformations Luke had begun to experience since arriving in Scream Street. Only one part of his body would change to that of a werewolf. This time it was his head.

A thin film spread across Luke's eyes and he found that he could now see more clearly in the darkness. Cleo was feeling for the torch while Resus pulled item after item from his cloak, searching for something with which to relight it.

A sound caused Luke's head to snap round. The man was in front of him, turning the dials on the front of the largest machine. Luke pounced, knocking him to the floor.

"Please don't hurt me!" the figure begged.

"Luke, stop!" yelled Resus. "I know that voice!"

A match hissed and the room was flooded with light as the torch burst into life. Cleo gasped.

Lying on the floor beneath Luke was Alston Negative.

Chapter Three
The Machine

Resus moved the torch closer. *"Dad?"*

Alston's eyes filled with tears. Blood had run down his fangs and onto his shirt front. "I'm… I'm sorry!" he said hoarsely. Sliding out from beneath Luke, he jumped to his feet and ran for the door.

"Dad!" Resus shouted again as Alston dashed

out of the room, his foot catching the block of concrete holding the door open. The older vampire was quickly lost from view as the metal door slammed shut. Resus didn't move.

"Are you OK?" asked Cleo.

Resus nodded. "At least we know what was bothering the rats now."

"Ra roar," growled Luke, his head still that of a werewolf.

Resus turned to face him. "What?"

"Roar rad rut ra roar," Luke snarled.

"I can't understand you."

"Roar rad rut ra roar!" repeated Luke.

Resus shook his head. "You sound like a cartoon dog."

Luke sighed and held up a hand, extending all five fingers.

"Charades!" said Cleo. "Luke's going to mime what he means!"

"This has got to be a nightmare," Resus moaned. "I'll wake up in a minute."

"OK, second word!" beamed Cleo as Luke folded over three of his fingers. They watched as Luke trotted around the room, flapping his arms out behind him.

"Er… Something that flies?" guessed Cleo. "A bird? A bat!"

"A total mentalist if you ask me," mumbled Resus.

Luke pointed to Resus with one hand and mimed long teeth with the fingers of his other.

"Fangs!" squealed Cleo with delight. "Vampire? Resus!" She followed Luke's silent instructions. "No, not Resus… Bigger. Resus's dad!"

Luke nodded furiously and held up the pinkie of his right hand.

"Fifth word," said Cleo, adding "door!" as Luke acted out opening a door and stepping through. "Right, third word! Sounds like foot. Er… Put? Mutt? Gut?" Luke closed his imaginary door again and again. "But? Cut?"

"It's *shut*!" roared Resus in frustration. "Shut! The sentence is: 'Your dad shut the door'." His eyes widened. "My dad shut the door?" He dashed across the room and pulled on the handle. The door was locked tight. "We're trapped."

"Trapped?" said Cleo. "How?"

"The latch must have dropped down on the other side," said Resus. "This is ridiculous! My dad needs help and we're stuck in here!" A crack echoed around the room and Luke buried his head in his hands, wincing as it began to shrink back from its werewolf form.

"We *all* need to get out, Resus," said Cleo calmly. "Luke's got to find the next relic to take his parents home."

"Oh, and while we're off on another adventure for wolf-boy, my dad's lying injured somewhere?" snapped Resus. "You saw the blood on his shirt!"

Luke glared at Resus as the thick fur disappeared back into his skin. "I don't need your help to find the next relic," he retorted. "I'll do it on my own."

"You couldn't find your way around *Everwell's* without me!" shouted Resus, kicking at the metal door.

"Of course! No one can do anything in Scream Street without permission from the all-powerful vampires!" yelled Luke.

Resus spun to face him. "You take that back. I'm warning you!"

Luke pretended to shake with fear. "Ooh, I've upset the scary vampire! Watch out, Cleo, he might throw his false teeth at you!"

Cleo leapt in between the boys. "Will you

two stop it?" she demanded. "Everyone's just a little wound up! We'll help your dad *and* find the next relic once we've worked out how to get out of here."

Luke and Resus glared at each other. A small squeak made them jump as a rat's nose appeared briefly through a hole at the bottom of the door. It sniffed at the air before quickly disappearing again.

Cleo crouched down to the tiny hole. "Look!" she said.

"My foot must have gone through the bottom of the door when I kicked it," said Resus. He produced a crowbar from inside his cloak and used it to break a piece of brittle metal away from the hole. "If the door has rusted enough, we *might* be able to break our way through…"

Resus scratched at the hole with the crowbar but could only widen it by a few centimetres. "We'll need more than just this to get through."

"We could tear parts off this machine," suggested Luke.

Resus handed the crowbar to Cleo and wedged the torch in the handle of the door. "Keep working on that," he said.

Luke walked around to the far side of the machine and found a loose strip of metal on the front of a control panel. Sliding his fingers underneath, he began to prise it away from its housing.

"I've got something," he said. "How about you?"

Resus didn't reply.

Luke sighed. "Look, I'm sorry for what I said about vampires," he began. But Resus appeared to have forgotten their argument.

"This is the blood filter!"

"The what?" said Luke.

"The machine I was telling you about last night," answered Resus. "It filters blood out of the waste water and pumps it into Scream Street. My dad must have known it was down here and come to try and fix it."

"And he didn't want to bite one of his family so he used the rats to keep him going," added Cleo. "That's why he had blood on his shirt!"

"He's turned to rats before," said Resus. "When my mum put him on a diet."

"But why did he panic like that when he saw us?" asked Luke.

Resus shrugged. "He might have thought we were—"

"Someone's coming!" hissed Cleo, joining Luke and Resus in the shadows. Resus blew out the torch, plunging the room into darkness.

The metal latch scraped as it was lifted, and slowly the door opened. Luke's breath caught in his throat as he saw who was standing there. Illuminated by a gas lamp was the landlord of Scream Street, Sir Otto Sneer.

Dixon, Sir Otto's nephew, wedged the concrete block against the door, his greasy ginger hair slapping against his thin cheeks.

Sir Otto, his face lit eerily by the gas lamp in his hands, blew smoke from his cigar and sniffed the air. "Someone's been here," he snarled.

"I know," replied Dixon.

Sir Otto glared at him. "*How* do you know?"

Dixon gestured towards the ageing machinery. "Someone had to bring this down here on purpose," he explained. "You'd never be able to flush something *this* size down the toilet. Although, I once did a poo so big that it almost didn't—"

"You moron!" shouted Sir Otto. "I meant, someone's been down here recently! It'll be one of the freaks, trying to restart the blood supply. Disable the machine. The food I jammed into the pipes won't block them for ever!"

Dixon stepped up to the machine and opened one of the metal covers. He grasped the edge of a dusty circuit board and began to pull. His fingers slipped in the grime and oil that covered it. "Can't … quite … get it…" he groaned.

"Then find me someone who can!" Sir Otto growled. "The sooner I send those vampires insane with bloodlust, the sooner they'll force the wolf-boy to give me the book in return for reconnecting the supply!"

In the darkness behind the machine, Resus opened his mouth to respond, but Luke held up a hand to silence his friend. They had to stay hidden.

"Someone else…" mumbled Dixon, closing his eyes. The skin on his face and hands began to ripple, like the surface of a pond in a breeze.

Luke watched as Sir Otto's nephew transformed. He'd known that Dixon was a shapeshifter but had never seen the process up close before. It looked effortless. So different from the awkwardness of Luke's own changes.

Within seconds, Dixon had become Bella Negative. Luke knew it wasn't really Resus's mum, but he had to grip his friend's arm tightly to prevent an outburst.

Bella's black-painted fingernails gripped the circuit board and pulled. The aged component shifted slightly, but it remained wedged inside the machine.

"Well, what did you expect?" demanded Sir Otto. "Those sharp-toothed idiots are useless at just about everything!" Luke clamped a hand over Resus's mouth.

"Now," continued the landlord, "change into someone who can actually achieve something!" There was a sound like milk being poured into a glass and Sir Otto found himself faced with an exact replica of himself.

"How's this, Uncle?"

"You're heading for a night in the dungeon," the real Sir Otto barked. "Just stop the blood before those stupid vampires figure out what's going on!"

Resus battled against Luke's grip. "That's all I can take," the vampire hissed. "I'm going to bite him until my fangs break!"

"Stop it!" whispered Luke. "We can't let them know we're here!"

But it was too late. As Dixon melted into the shape of a giant Egyptian mummy, Cleo shrieked. "You're not fit to wear his bandages!"

Chapter Four
The Escape

"I'm sorry!" panted Cleo as she, Luke and Resus raced back along the sewer tunnel. "I couldn't help myself!"

Luke scowled at the mummy. "I spent all that time keeping Resus quiet, when I should have had my hand clamped over *your* mouth!"

A crash came from behind them and the trio sped up. "That'll be Dixon breaking the door down," said Resus. He had slammed it shut behind them, but the act had bought only a few seconds' head start.

"After them!" roared Sir Otto, his voice echoing off the stone walls.

Cleo reached the ladder that led back up to Everwell's Emporium, but Luke grabbed her arm as she placed a foot on the bottom rung. "No," he said. "We'll just let them *think* we've gone back up there."

The trio crouched in the darkness further along the tunnel as Dixon, still in the form of the Cleo's father, dashed into view.

Cleo jumped to her feet and opened her mouth to call out.

Resus leapt up and tackled her to the ground, clamping his cape over her mouth. "Will you keep quiet?" he hissed.

Dixon clambered up the ladder and disappeared as Sir Otto, sweating heavily and out of breath, arrived. The landlord placed the circuit board on the floor and, with a great deal of effort, followed his nephew.

 43

"Looks like he disabled the machine after all," said Resus.

Luke nodded. "He won't want to take it into the emporium until he knows who's up there."

"What now?" whispered Resus.

"Stay hidden until Sir Otto's gone," said Luke.

"Mmph fmmph feemfeem mph?" mumbled Cleo.

"Oops, sorry!" said Resus, climbing off his friend and helping her to sit up.

"Do you think Eefa will give us away?" asked Cleo.

Resus shook his head. "She hates Sir Otto as much as the rest of Scream Street does. Eefa won't tell him anything."

The trio remained hidden in the dark as a muffled row erupted in the emporium above them. "Where are they?" roared Sir Otto.

"I don't know who you're talking about," shouted Eefa. "No one's been up or down that ladder in weeks!"

"Eefa's covering for us," whispered Luke. "We're safe."

"The freaks are sticking together," said Sir Otto. "We'll never find them now. Get your new

44

toy and we'll go somewhere where the company is better."

"New toy?" asked Dixon. "It's not my birthday."

"You idiot," bellowed the landlord. "I mean the item we've just acquired!"

The mummified shape of Niles Farr reached down through the hatch as Dixon finally realized that Sir Otto was referring to the blood filter's circuit board.

Cleo leapt to her feet. "I'll feed you to the Sphinx!"

Resus groaned. "Here we go again…"

"They're still down there, Uncle Otto!" Dixon yelled as Luke, Resus and Cleo raced further down the tunnel.

"I'll throw you into the Nile!" Cleo screamed over her shoulder.

"We need to talk about managing your anger!" Resus shouted, as he pulled a jar of tiny glowing insects from his cloak.

"What are those supposed to be?" scoffed Cleo.

"Fireflies," replied Resus. "I left my last torch back behind the blood filter."

"We can't find our way through the sewers with fireflies!"

"Well, unless you can do any better, they're all we've got," said Resus.

The trio suddenly found a metal gate blocking their way. Luke rattled the gate; it barely moved. "We've run out of sewer," he said.

Sir Otto's voice echoed along the tunnel. "We can't be far behind them!"

"What do we do now?" asked Luke.

"We fight," said Resus.

"Fight?" demanded Cleo. "With what? Your jar of shiny wasps?"

"We've got a werewolf," said Resus, pointing to Luke in the dim light. "All we have to do is make him angry and there's no more Dixon!"

"Er, excuse me…" said Luke.

"No, Resus!" Cleo yelled. "I can't watch him tear my dad to pieces!"

"He's *not* your dad!" snapped Resus.

"Can I just…?"

"I know that!" came the reply. "But he'll *look* like my dad while Luke's ripping his arms off! How am I supposed to deal with that?"

"Can I say something?" asked Luke.

"What?" barked Resus and Cleo together.

"I'm not ripping *anyone's* arms off, if you don't mind! I'm not some sort of fur-covered weapon to be unleashed whenever we're in trouble!"

Footsteps approached. Dixon was almost upon them.

"Then I'm out of ideas," Resus sighed. "It's not as if an escape route is going to appear out of thin air."

As Luke opened his mouth to reply, a handful of bricks crumbled from the sewer wall, revealing a green, cracked face behind them. "Little dudes!" the zombie beamed. "What are you doing here?"

"Looking for a way out, Doug," said Resus. "Can you help us?"

"No problemo, tiny vampire!" grinned Doug, climbing out of the hole. He turned and called back into the tunnel from which he had appeared. "Turf! Back up, dude. We got us some new passengers on the party train!"

Within seconds Luke, Resus and Cleo were crawling through the tunnel of earth behind a larger zombie, Turf. The monster paused every

few seconds to giggle at something the trio could neither see nor hear.

"Don't worry about Turf, little dudes," said Doug as he collapsed the tunnel behind them. "It's this rich soil – it goes straight to his head!"

"Where exactly does this tunnel lead?" asked Resus.

In the soft glow provided by the fireflies, Doug grinned, revealing rotten teeth that crawled with maggots and lice. "The party train goes wherever there's good times to be had, my man!"

"Then I think we should head for my house," said Luke. "We'll see if Mr Skipstone knows how to restore the blood supply for your dad."

"Thanks," said Resus, smiling gratefully. "Thirteen Scream Street, Doug."

"Thirteen it is!" grinned the zombie. "Turf, hang a left at the next set of tree roots."

Turf, however, was no longer paying attention, preferring instead to watch a passing worm with an expression of amazed delight.

"I knew I shouldn't have let Turf tunnel today," said Doug. "He was up all night downing brain smoothies." The zombie fixed the trio with a steady gaze. "Let this be a lesson to you, little dudes. Friends don't let friends drink and dig!"

A zombie's fist burst through the lawn in the back garden of 13 Scream Street, its yellow, weeping sores glinting in the moonlight. A second fist appeared, pushing soil and grass to one side, widening the hole. A head was forced up into the cool air, flakes of dead skin dropping from it like decomposing dandruff.

"This is your stop, dudes," announced Doug as he clambered to his feet. "Thirteen Scream

 49

Street!" The zombie helped Luke, Resus and Cleo out of the hole.

"Keep an eye open for trouble," Luke called back to the other two as he disappeared into the house. "I'll run up and get Mr Skipstone."

Resus reached inside his cloak and pulled out an old bottle filled with swirling white liquid. He held it out to their zombie rescuer. "This is to say thanks for helping us."

Doug took the bottle and blew the dust from the label. "Spinal fluid!" he beamed. "Dude, how did you know?"

Resus shrugged, embarrassed. "I got talking to some zombies at my cousin's wedding, and they swore by the stuff. I thought I'd pick you guys up a bottle."

"Turf!" Doug yelled into the tunnel. "Get up here and see this!" The zombie grasped the scabby green arm that extended up from the hole and pulled, tumbling backwards as the limb ripped away at the shoulder.

"Man!" Doug said, tossing the arm back into the hole. "You are *so* wasted!"

As Doug disappeared the way they had come, Luke reappeared at the back door, tucking the silver book into his pocket.

Cleo was examining her reflection in the glass of the living-room window. "I'm running out of clean bandages," she moaned, trying to wipe away the worst of the dirt and grass stains. "This will never—"

She was interrupted by a scream above her. Mr and Mrs Watson stood at their bedroom window.

"It's OK!" Luke shouted up. "It's just me, Resus and Cleo!"

Mrs Watson shook her head and pointed beyond her son with a trembling hand. Luke spun round and saw that the lawn had turned black. Hundreds of rats were slowly advancing towards them.

"Where did they come from?" shrieked Cleo.

"You tell me," replied Luke. "You were the one watching for trouble."

"I-I didn't see them," stammered Cleo.

"Oh, no…" breathed Resus, glancing at the window behind him.

"That's not a good 'Oh, no', is it," said Luke, his eyes fixed on the sharp teeth of the rodents at the front of the pack.

Resus shook his head. "If Cleo didn't see

 51

their reflections in the window, there's only one explanation…"

"What?" demanded Cleo.

"They're vampire rats!"

Chapter Five
The Cat

"**Vampire rats?**" exclaimed Luke. "You never said there was such a thing as vampire rats!"

"There isn't," said Resus. "Or, at least, there *wasn't*! Some of the rats my dad bit must have got away. They've passed on the Energy."

"Energy? What energy?" asked Luke.

"Vampire Energy, with a capital 'E'," explained Resus. "When a vampire bites something, or someone, he transfers a little of his genetic code to the victim, creating another vampire."

"So, this Energy could spread through every rat in Scream Street?"

"I'd be surprised if it hasn't already," said Resus.

"What's brought them to the surface?" asked Cleo. "You sent that black—"

A sharp hiss turned their attention to the top of the garden wall. The cat Resus had pulled from his cloak was glaring down at them with red eyes, the blood of some poor defenceless animal dripping from its freshly grown fangs. The creature had doubled in size and now resembled a sleek panther, its muscles rippling as it stalked along the wall. The rats closest to it squealed and raced away, digging their way furiously under the gate to escape.

"Oh…" said Luke.

"Aww!" said Cleo.

"Aww?" asked Resus.

"I was just picturing it in a little cape, like yours," said Cleo.

"Are you out of your pyramid?" said Resus. "My dad's spawning deadly new species that'll rip out your throat for fun, and you want to dress them up?"

Cleo shrugged. "I like cats," she replied flatly.

"Well, I wouldn't try to pet that one," said Resus. "You'll end up a few fingers short!"

"Nonsense," said Cleo. "A cat's a cat. I have a bond with them." She stepped forward and held out her hand.

"Cleo, no!" snapped Luke.

"Get back!" hissed Resus.

"Here, boy," called Cleo softly. "Come and prove to these two wimps that you're not dangerous." The cat leapt down from the wall and crept towards her hand. It sniffed her bandaged

fingers for a moment before licking their tips.

"There!" said Cleo. "I told you there was nothing to—"

The cat pounced, fangs bared as it clawed its way towards Cleo's throat. The mummy screamed and fell backwards, trying to knock the cat off her chest.

"Don't let it bite her!" shouted Resus. "She'll become a vampire mummy!"

"A *what*?" demanded Luke.

"Something that's likely to bite you, then bandage the wound itself," yelled Resus. "We have to help her!"

Luke scanned the garden for a possible weapon and his eyes fell on a rake. He dashed across the lawn to grab it. Raising it high above his head, he raced back across the grass with a roar and brought it down as hard as he could.

With the vampire Energy heightening its already keen senses, the cat saw the danger and leapt off Cleo just in time. The metal prongs of the rake impaled themselves deep into the mummy's chest.

"What are you doing?" exclaimed Resus. He pushed Luke to one side and pulled at the rake. It was stuck fast. Luke grabbed hold of the handle and they both tugged, but the tool wouldn't move.

Cleo glared up at them. "It's a good job my internal organs were removed before I was mummified, or that could have done more than just hurt!" she snapped.

"Where's the cat?" asked Resus warily.

"Over by the gate," said Luke. "I think we've scared it."

"Scared it?" yelled Cleo. "I'm surprised it's not wetting itself! If that's what you do to your friends, Luke Watson, what do you do to your enemies?"

"I'm sorry!" protested Luke. "I was trying to help."

"Well, next time – don't," barked Cleo. "I can take care of myself!"

"Yeah," teased Resus as he pressed a foot onto Cleo's chest and finally managed to extract the rake. "It looks like it!"

"What now?" asked Luke as Cleo clambered to her feet and rearranged her bandages to hide the holes in her chest. The vampire cat stalked around the perimeter of the garden, its scarlet

eyes never leaving the children.

"We have to stop it biting anyone and passing on the Energy," said Resus.

"Can we frighten it back down to the sewers?" suggested Luke.

"How?" asked Resus.

"I don't know," said Luke. "What are vampires scared of?"

Resus looked blank.

"What's your dad scared of?"

"My mum says he's scared of housework…"

"Brilliant!" snorted Luke. "We'll tell the killer cat it's down to do the dishes tonight, and then it'll disappear. Problem solved!" Resus reddened.

"What about garlic?" said Cleo. "Aren't vampires afraid of garlic?"

"It might work," said Resus. "My dad won't have the stuff in the house."

"Perfect!" said Cleo. "Let's have a look in your cloak."

The vampire shook his head. "If my mum got a whiff of it, I'd be grounded for a year." A smile spread across his face. "But I do know someone who grows the stuff, and he's just a couple of houses along."

"How do we get past the cat?" asked Luke.

Resus pulled a large chunk of meat from inside his cloak and smiled. "Leave that to me!"

Luke dropped to his knees and began to dig in the soil with his fingers.

Cleo was staring up at Resus in disgust. "Whose liver was that?"

"What do you mean?"

"Resus," said Cleo, "I'm a mummy. I keep my insides on the outside. I know a liver when I see it!"

"It was my nan's," sighed Resus. "She left it to me in her will."

Cleo shuddered. "And you've carried it around in your cloak ever since?"

"It distracted the vampire cat long enough for us to get over the wall, didn't it?" retorted Resus.

Luke pulled a cream-coloured bulb from the soil. "Is this it?" he asked. "I've only ever seen garlic in supermarkets before."

Resus sniffed the bulb. "Yep," he said, wrinkling up his nose. "That's garlic!"

"Well," said Cleo, "time to test it out – unless

Resus has any other bits of his family tucked away somewhere."

Luke crushed the garlic bulb in his hand. Taking aim, he hurled the fistful of cloves at the black cat. To his delight, it hissed angrily and backed away.

"It works!" he beamed, pushing his hands back into the soil. "Let's get some more of it and we can—"

Two large, scuffed leather boots appeared in his line of vision. "What do you finks you're doin'?" growled a deep voice.

Luke's gaze travelled upwards past a pair of thick hairy legs to a frilly pink tutu. A pot belly hung, wobbling, over the top of the skirt and two large tattooed arms ended beside the gut in massive fists. Stubble coated the chin of the rough-skinned face that was glowering down at Luke. Above it, a close-cropped haircut was topped off with a delicate tiara.

"I saids, what you doin'?"

"Er, Luke," said Resus as brightly as he could. "This is Twinkle." He slowly pushed a newly exposed bulb back into the soil. "And this is his garlic."

Luke swallowed hard. "P-pleased to meet you."

"I needs that garlic," snarled Twinkle. "I uses it to make me fairy dust!"

Luke stared. This was a *fairy*? He looked more like a bricklayer in fancy dress.

"Sorry, Twinkle," said Resus. "We would have asked, but we've got a bit of a problem." He gestured towards the cat, watching warily from the safety of the garden wall.

Twinkle sniffed. "What's that fing?"

"A vampire cat," explained Cleo.

Twinkle nodded slowly. Luke was certain that, if he were able to get close enough, he would hear the cogs moving inside the fairy's brain. Eventually, Twinkle said, "What d'you needs me to do?"

Resus handed the fairy the garlic he had just unearthed. "Take garlic to every house in Scream Street except mine," he said. "Hang a piece on each door and tell everyone to stay inside until it's safe."

Twinkle's granite expression hardened even further. "Gotcha!" He bent to pull the rest of the bulbs out of the soil and shoved them into a pink bag that hung at his side. Straightening, the fairy flapped a pair of delicate wings, floated gently off the ground and soared away over the rooftops.

"I never would have…" began Luke, before

a vicious yowl sent a shiver up his spine. The vampire cat was slinking towards them again.

Cleo swallowed hard. "I think maybe we should have kept a little bit of that garlic for ourselves!"

Chapter Six
The Witch

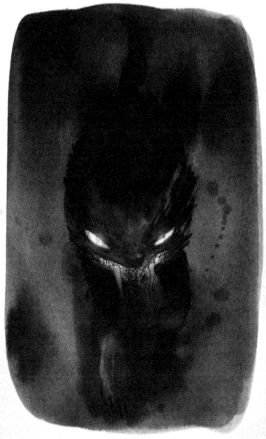

The cat crawled across the garden, fangs bared.

"Can you fight it, Luke?" asked Resus. "I know you don't want to be considered a

weapon or anything, but you might be our only chance."

Luke shook his head as they backed away. "I doubt I'd have enough time to transfor—"

There was a crash as he tumbled over a lawn-mower. *Skipstone's Tales of Scream Street* fell from his pocket and landed on the grass.

The cat saw its chance and leapt. Luke covered his face with his hands.

"Shan! Leave them alone!"

The cat paused, surprised for a moment by the unexpected voice. Then it shook its head to clear the sound and raced for Luke once more.

"SHAN! NO!"

The effect upon the vampire cat was instant. It rolled onto its back and mewed gently, all thoughts of attacking Luke lost.

"Who said that?" asked Resus.

"I did," came the reply. "And you had better have a very good reason for infecting my cat with vampire Energy!"

The trio looked down. The voice was com-ing from *Skipstone's Tales of Scream Street*, now lying open on the lawn. An image began to form among the scrawled handwriting. A pencil sketch appeared and grew in size, as though someone was running towards the book from the other side.

The paper began to stretch as the figure rose from the page. Long charcoal hair swished in the gentle breeze of the garden and slim, black-nailed fingers gripped the diamond-studded handle of a razor-sharp knife.

"Get back inside this book right now!" ordered Samuel Skipstone. The silver cover of *Skipstone's Tales of Scream Street* tried to close over the foot of the woman, still on the page from which she had appeared.

"I will do no such thing until this monster leaves Shan alone!" roared the

illustration. She grabbed a handful of Luke's hair, paper crinkling.

"He's no monster," said Skipstone. "That's the werewolf I told you about."

"*This* is the boy who wishes to open a doorway and take his parents out of Scream Street? I ought to cast a spell and keep them here for ever!"

"A spell?" gasped Luke. "You're a *witch*?"

"Not *a* witch, darling," replied the sketch. "*The* witch! Nelly Twist, the very first witch in Scream Street."

"I– I'm Luke Watson."

"Well, Luke Watson," said Nelly Twist. "If you expect me to provide you with the relic you seek, you must first do something for me."

"OK," said Luke. "Anything!"

Nelly Twist swung the diamond-handled knife towards Luke. "Kill my cat."

Luke stared up at the witch in terror. "Are you serious?"

The illustration of Nelly Twist tightened her grip on Luke's hair. "Deadly serious," she hissed. "Now, take the knife and kill my cat!"

"Nelly, stop this," demanded Samuel Skip-stone. "He's just a boy!"

67

"If he wants my help, he must prove himself worthy," insisted the witch. "If he refuses to do my bidding, he will not get my relic and his quest is at an end."

Swallowing hard, Luke took the drawing of the dagger from the witch's outstretched hand. As his fingers touched it, blue sparks flashed across the illustration and the knife became real. He turned the blade down towards the black cat sitting quietly at the witch's feet.

"Luke Watson, if you do this I'll never speak to you again!" shouted Cleo.

Luke gazed up through horror-filled eyes at Nelly Twist, hoping this was nothing more than a test to see how far he would go. The witch's pencil-lined face remained stern. "Do it, or your parents will never leave Scream Street!"

Cleo turned away, shaking, as Luke raised the knife over the cat. Resus could not tear his gaze from the horrible scene.

Screwing his eyes shut, Luke plunged the knife down. There was a small yowl, then silence. Only Cleo's sobs could be heard over the rustle of paper as the witch took the knife from Luke's hand.

"Look!" said Resus.

"Stop it!" yelled Cleo.

"I mean it," said Resus. "Look at the cat!"

Luke opened his eyes and watched in amazement as, slowly, the body of the cat rose into the air and began to spin, as though caught in the midst of a tiny tornado. The animal began to blur, shifting in and out of focus.

After a moment, the spinning slowed and a smaller, very much alive cat drifted to the ground. It mewed softly and padded over to the witch, licking her paper hand, no vampire fangs to be seen.

"That's impossible!" said Resus.

"Not for Shan," explained Nelly. "Many years ago he wriggled his way into my store cupboard and ate the raw ingredients to dozens of potions. They mixed in his stomach and he remains alive to this day."

"You mean, he'll live for ever?" gasped Cleo.

"Not quite," said the witch. "He accidentally increased his number of lives from nine to nine hundred and ninety-nine. I believe he's just embarked on number one hundred and forty-one now." She turned to Luke. "He would have

suffered greatly throughout his latest life had you not ended it. Thank you for killing my cat."

"You're welcome," said Luke as the witch helped him to stand. "I think!"

"Who has been looking after Shan while I've been away?" asked Nelly.

Resus raised a hand. "I've known him since I was a toddler. My mum used to give him milk at the back door. One day I was playing in the garden and he went to sleep inside my cape. He seemed comfortable, so I let him stay there."

"Then you are to be thanked as well, young vampire," said Nelly. "It is not easy to care for your pets when you are no longer alive."

"How can we be talking to you if you're dead?" asked Cleo.

"Technically, you're talking to my memory of Nelly Twist," said Samuel Skipstone from the cover of the book. "I should add that I do not wholly approve of the spell you are using to do this, Nelly!"

"You always were a worrier, Samuel," laughed the witch. "I had to be sure this boy was worthy of my gift."

"Could you show us the clue again, please?"

Luke asked the book. Skipstone smiled and brought the riddle into view on the page.

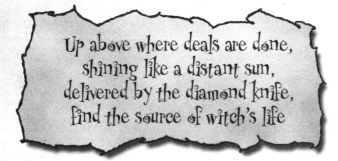

Up above where deals are done,
shining like a distant sun,
delivered by the diamond knife,
find the source of witch's life

Luke looked up at the illustrated witch. "*The source of witch's life*. That's your blood, isn't it?" Nelly Twist nodded.

"You're just going to give me some?" said Luke, eyeing the knife again.

"If you were to cut me now, all you would find would be the ink from Skipstone's pen," said Nelly. "I drew my blood a long time ago and it is hidden from those who do not deserve it." As she spoke, her fingertips began to fade.

"What's happening?" asked Cleo.

"The spell is wearing off," said Nelly as her arms vanished into clouds of pencil dust. "We do not have much time." She fixed Luke's eyes with her own. "You are certain you wish to help your parents leave Scream Street?"

Luke nodded. "I just want them to be happy."

"And you, Luke Watson? What will make you happy?"

Luke glanced from Cleo to Resus, then back up at the outline of Nelly Twist's face, suspended in the air. "Taking my family home."

"Very well," said Nelly as the final pencil line was dragged back into the book. "Shan, show them where to find my blood."

The witch's voice echoed away into silence. Her cat padded to the garden gate and sat, watching Luke.

"He wants you to follow him," said Cleo.

Resus stooped to pick up *Skipstone's Tales of Scream Street*. He closed the book and handed it to Luke. "Ready?" he asked.

Luke nodded and the trio made for the gate, stopping as a familiar green fist punched up through the soil in front of them. Doug's head followed as the hole widened. Resus stared. Something wasn't right.

"What's that?" gasped Cleo, pointing to the zombie's cheek. A rat was clamped onto the side of Doug's face, teeth buried deep in his dead, cracked flesh. The zombie ripped the rat away, losing a chunk of skin in the process. The rodent squealed as it was hurled over the garden wall.

"Doug, are you OK?" asked Luke, crouching down next to him. He froze as he saw two glistening fangs push their way into the zombie's broken smile.

"Never better, little dude!" beamed Doug, licking his new teeth with a long black tongue and eyeing Luke's throat. "Although I sure am thirsty!"

Chapter Seven
The Relic

Luke, Resus and Cleo raced along Scream Street with the witch's cat. Doug chased after them, licking his new fangs and shouting, "Blood, dudes!"

"The zombies in my computer games never move this fast," panted Luke.

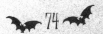

"It's the vampire Energy," explained Resus. "It heightens the senses."

"So does the threat of having your throat bitten!" said Luke.

"Do my ears deceive me, or did you just crack a joke?" asked Resus.

"I've got just as good a sense of humour as you," said Luke. "The difference is, my material doesn't stink!"

"Something *does* stink, though," said Cleo, sniffing. "I smell garlic."

"There's Twinkle's bag!" exclaimed Resus, hurrying to pick up the pink sack.

"Why didn't he hand the stuff out, like you asked?" said Luke.

"There's your answer," replied Resus, pointing to the fairy as he stumbled out of a nearby garden, blood dripping from his newly sprouted fangs.

"A vampire fairy," laughed Luke. "You wouldn't want one of those on top of your Christmas tree."

"Shan's leading us to the square," said Cleo, as the black cat raced ahead.

Resus glanced over his shoulder as Twinkle joined Doug to lumber after them.

"I say we follow him!" he quipped.

As they reached the central square, the trio stopped dead. Dozens of the street's residents were milling about, each sporting razor-sharp teeth. At the sight of the uninfected children, they turned and slowly advanced upon them.

"There's no way out!" said Cleo.

"Yes, there is," said Resus. "Up!" From inside his cloak he pulled a length of rope with a metal grappling hook on the end and threw it onto the roof of Everwell's Emporium. With a satisfying *clink* it lodged firmly behind the chimney. "Come on!" he shouted, tugging on the rope.

Luke didn't move. He was rooted to the spot, staring into the advancing crowd. Among them, fangs glinting in the moonlight, was his dad. Luke started towards him but Resus pulled him back. "Are you crazy?"

"But, my dad…"

"We'll find a way to help him once we're safe," said Resus. "Now, climb!"

Luke went first, followed by Cleo with Shan tucked under her arm. Resus landed a kick into a vampire bog monster's snarling face and brought up the rear.

Luke was just pulling himself up onto the roof when he heard Cleo shout, "The book!" Resus made a grab for *Skipstone's Tales of Scream Street* as it fell from Luke's pocket above him, but he missed. The book landed with a clatter among the ravenous residents below.

"I have to get it!" yelled Luke as Cleo and Resus dragged themselves up onto the roof beside him. Luke's dad was already climbing up the rope.

Resus plunged his hand into the bag of garlic and pulled out a clove to throw. Luke grabbed his wrist. "What do you think you're doing?"

"If your dad bites you, you'll be a vampire werewolf – virtually unstoppable," said Resus. "You could end up really hurting him, or worse!"

Luke sighed and took the garlic from Resus. "I'm sorry," he whispered. As the clove hit Mr Watson's forehead, he screamed in pain and fell from the rope, landing among the hungry crowd.

Resus pulled up the rope and stared down at the swarm of Scream Street residents, all reaching up towards the trio, calling for their blood. He caught a flash of silver as *Skipstone's Tales of Scream Street* was kicked around.

"We've got to get them away from the book, or Mr Skipstone will be trampled!" he said, throwing more of the garlic at the crowd below. Each time the vampire residents were hit, they screamed in agony, clawing at where the garlic had made contact with their skin.

"It's hurting them, but they're not leaving!" shouted Luke over the cries of the hungry horde. "We'll have to find another way!" As he spoke, Shan ran past him and leapt off the rooftop.

"Shan!" screamed Cleo, but the small cat was already on the ground, racing away across the square. The mob turned and chased after him as the smell of fresh blood reached them.

"He's done it," said Resus. "He's leading them away!"

Before long only one resident, a gargoyle, remained in the square. He bent to retrieve *Skipstone's Tales of Scream Street*.

"Excuse me, sir," called Luke. "That belongs to me!"

The gargoyle looked up, his face rippling as he transformed back into the gangly shape of Dixon. "Not any more, it doesn't!" the ginger-haired figure teased. "Uncle Otto will double my

pocket money for finding this!" Giggling to himself, Dixon skipped off towards the gates of Sneer Hall.

Luke slumped back onto the roof. "We've lost the book," he groaned.

"And Shan," added Cleo.

A smile slowly spread across Resus's face. "But," he said, "I think we've found the witch's blood."

The grappling hook caught in the guttering on the third attempt. "Got it!" grinned Resus, pulling the rope taut. It stretched between Everwell's Emporium and the house on the end of a nearby side street. In the sky between the two, a glittering glass vial hung, magically suspended in the air.

"Up above where deals are done," said Resus. "That was the first part of the clue. There used to be a market in the square every week before Sir Otto banned it. Deals were done then."

"I still don't get the next part," admitted Cleo. *"Shining like a distant sun."*

"The sun is a star," explained Luke. "From below, the vial of blood would look like any other star in the sky. We only saw it because we were up here."

"The perfect hiding place," said Resus. "In full view of everyone!" He secured the other end of the rope around the chimney.

"I still don't see why it has to be you that goes out there to get the relic," complained Cleo. "I'm the lightest."

Resus glanced at Luke, who was trying hard to ignore the cries of agony that indicated another resident's recruitment to the vampire cause.

"I want you to keep an eye on Luke," said Resus. "It's not easy to accept that your dad is a vampire."

"You manage OK," said Cleo.

"I've had longer to get used to it than he has," Resus smiled.

Cleo squeezed his hand. "Be careful!" she whispered.

Resus nodded. He walked to the edge of the

rooftop and glanced down. Clutching a broom handle to balance himself, the vampire stepped onto the rope.

Luke watched with concern as his friend walked slowly towards the vial of blood. He hadn't wanted Resus to put himself in danger to get the relic, but the vampire had insisted.

"Hey!" Resus called. "If being a vampire doesn't work out, there's always a career in the circus waiting for me!"

"Just concentrate!" Luke hissed.

Resus stuck out his tongue in defiance and spun on the rope like a ballerina before continuing.

He reached the spot directly beneath the vial and, holding the broom handle in one hand, stretched up with the other to grab it. His

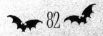

fingers grazed the bottom of the vial teasingly, but it remained suspended in the air.

"I can't … quite … get it," said Resus. "I'll have to stand on my toes."

"Be careful!" called Luke, gripping the rope.

Resus tucked the wooden pole under his arm and stepped up onto his toes, reaching with his free hand. His fingers found the glass jar and he pulled it towards him, breaking the spell that had held it there for so long.

"I've got it!" he shouted triumphantly. "One witch's relic coming up!"

Suddenly the rope wobbled violently and Resus had to thrust his arms out to keep his balance. The wooden pole fell, clattering to the ground. Luke looked over the square to the other end of the rope.

"It's the gutter!" squealed Cleo. "It's collapsing!"

Section by section, the old gutter holding the hook tore away from the other rooftop. The rope jerked hard again and Resus slipped. His stomach hit the rope and he bounced back into the air before falling to one side. Grabbing the rope with his free hand, he swung high above the ground.

"Resus!" yelled Luke. "Pull yourself along the rope to me!"

"But, the blood…" called Resus, still clutching the vial.

"Never mind the blood!" Luke shrieked. "Just get back here!"

More of the guttering fell away. "Resus!" Cleo screamed.

"No!" roared Luke as the rope dipped dramatically. Resus clung on tightly, but Luke could see the terror in his eyes.

"Luke!" the vampire shouted. "Catch!" Swinging his arm, Resus threw the vial of blood towards his friend. Luke leapt to his feet and just managed to catch it before it could smash onto the roof of Everwell's Emporium.

Suddenly there was a splintering sound from

across the square. The gutter opposite finally collapsed and Resus fell.

Luke and Cleo scrambled to the edge of the
roof and stared disbelievingly at the vampire's
body as it lay in an expanding pool of blood
below.

Chapter Eight
The Plan

"He's alive," said Eefa Everwell as she laid Resus on the shop counter and dabbed at the gash on his forehead with a cloth. "He's lost a lot of blood, though."

"It should have been me," sobbed Cleo, tears soaking into her bandages. "I'm the one who does stupid things and gets hurt – not Resus!"

Luke put his arm around the mummy's shoulders, watching as Eefa cleaned Resus's wound. He and Cleo had slid down the rope to reach their friend, keeping a watchful eye for any Energy-infected resident who might take the opportunity to grab a quick snack. There had been no garlic left to protect them.

Hammering on the shop door, Luke had insisted that Eefa open her mouth and show him her teeth to prove she hadn't been turned into a vampire too. Now all he could do was watch as the witch tended to Resus.

"Is there anything you can do?" he asked nervously.

Eefa shrugged. "If my blood supply was running, I could replace what he'd lost and cast a charm on the plasma so that it matched his blood type."

Luke pulled up the sleeve of his top and offered his arm to the witch. "Take some from me."

Eefa shook her head. "The spell won't work on fresh blood. His system would produce antibodies to fight it and it could make his condition a lot worse."

She gazed down at the unconscious vampire. "Even a small amount of older blood would do, but we just don't have any."

Luke pulled the witch's vial from his pocket. "Yes, we do."

Resus opened his eyes and looked around him. He was lying on the floor of Everwell's Emporium, a wall-hanging depicting the battle of Saint George and the Dragon covering him like a blanket. Cleo and Luke stood over by the counter, deep in quiet conversation with Eefa.

The vampire tried to sit up and discovered a pain in his head like he'd never felt before. In fact, now that he'd moved, it seemed to be in every part of his body. "That's the first time I've ever had an all-over headache!" he announced.

Luke and Cleo hurried over, delighted to see their friend awake.

"How are you?" asked Luke.

"My aches have got aches of their own," smiled Resus. "What happened?"

"I'll tell you what happened!" shouted Cleo. "You're a total idiot – that's what happened!" She began to slap Resus's chest with her bandaged hands. "You should never have been out on that rope! It should have been me!"

"Whoa, whoa!" cried Resus as Luke pulled Cleo off him.

"I thought we'd lost you," sobbed Cleo, hugging Resus tightly. Every muscle in the vampire's body hurt from the embrace, but he decided to keep quiet.

"You cut your head pretty badly," explained Luke. Resus reached up and felt the bandage around his forehead. "You lost a lot of blood."

"Blood!" said Resus, remembering. "Did you catch the witch's blood?"

Luke nodded. "You made me run for it, though," he smiled.

"Where is it now?" asked Resus.

Luke felt the empty crystal vial in his pocket. "Somewhere safe," he said, exchanging a glance with Cleo.

"What's going on?" Resus asked.

"Well," began Luke, "like I said, you lost a lot of blood…"

"And the supply is still disconnected…"

Resus's eyes widened as realization dawned. "I've got witch blood inside me?" he demanded.

 89

"How could you let that happen?"

"We didn't have much of a choice!"

"But ... *witch* blood," repeated Resus.

"What exactly is wrong with having witch blood inside you?" came Eefa's voice from across the shop.

"Nothing – if you're a witch!" snapped Resus, throwing the wall-hanging to one side and getting unsteadily to his feet.

"There wasn't time to send out for supplies," said Luke. "You were badly hurt. We had to do something straight away!"

"Eefa used a spell to expand the blood from the vial so that it replaced what you had lost," added Cleo. "She saved your life, Resus. You should be grateful!"

"I *am* grateful," said Resus. "Of course I am! It's just that..." He took a deep breath. "There was precious little of me that was genuine vampire to begin with. Now even some of that has been replaced."

"It was either lose the witch blood, or lose you," explained Luke. "Besides – just about everyone in Scream Street is more of a vampire than you right now!"

Resus ignored Luke's attempt to cheer him up. "You needed that blood," he said. "You needed it to open a doorway out of Scream Street."

"I know exactly where it is when I need it," replied Luke.

"But how can you get it back?" asked Resus.

Luke shrugged. "We'll cross that bridge when we come to it."

Resus stared. "You gave me the blood that you need to take your family home without knowing whether or not you could get it back?"

Luke handed Resus his cape. "You'd have done the same for me."

A feeling of light-headedness swept over Resus and he was forced to grip onto a nearby shelving unit for support. "You shouldn't be up and about yet," insisted Eefa. "You need rest."

"I haven't got time to rest," said Resus. "Sir Otto has *Skipstone's Tales of Scream Street* and we need to restart the blood supply to save my dad."

"My dad too," added Luke. "Before he gets too much of a taste for it."

"But the spell I used isn't perfect," said Eefa worriedly. "There could be some unwanted side effects…"

Resus took the witch's hand in his. "I'll be fine," he promised. "And thank you for everything. But we've got to get inside Sneer Hall."

"That might not be as easy as it sounds." Cleo was standing at the shop window, staring out into the central square. Luke and Resus joined her. The pack of vampire rats was back, hungrily lapping up the pool of blood Resus had left on the ground.

"I suppose I should be annoyed," said Resus. "That *is* my blood, after all."

"How are we going to get past them?" asked Luke. "They're right between us and Sir Otto's mansion."

"There's something else out there," said Cleo, her face pressed against the glass. A dark figure crept out of the bushes and crossed the square. "It's Shan!"

The cat looked directly at Cleo, then over at the vampire rats. Pulling its ears back flat against its head, it mewed softly.

"No!" screamed Cleo as the rats spun round. Within seconds the pack was on the cat, biting, tearing and scratching. Shan's tortured screams echoed around the square. "He didn't fight back!" she said. "He just stood there and let them—"

A sudden flash of red light stopped Cleo in her tracks and forced her, Luke and Resus to shield their eyes. When they looked back out into the square, a large cat with burning red eyes and sharp fangs was walking towards the Emporium.

"I know what he's doing!" yelled Cleo and she dashed for the shop door. The bat above the doorway screeched as she raced outside.

"CLEO!" roared Resus as he watched her approach the vampire cat, hand held out nervously. He held his breath as Shan licked at her fingers then, to his amazement, sat beside the mummy and softly rubbed up against her leg.

"It's safe to come out!"

called Cleo joyfully. Resus and Luke cautiously joined her beside Shan.

"Are you sure about this?" asked Luke as he and Resus picked their way through the vampire rats. The rodents ignored them, instead lining up in ranks behind Shan and Cleo.

"Perfectly sure," smiled the mummy. "They're on our side now."

The trio faced Sir Otto's mansion, a huge, sprawling building that took up an entire side of the square. "So," said Resus, "what's the plan?"

Luke cracked his knuckles. "We get inside Sneer Hall, rescue Mr Skipstone, find the missing piece of the blood filter, restart the blood supply and find a way to turn all the residents back to normal."

Resus fastened his cape back around his shoulders. "Not much, then?"

Luke shook his head. "Nah!"

Chapter Nine
The Light

The gates to Sneer Hall buckled. Luke smiled. It was incredible what the combined weight of almost a thousand rats could achieve.

The trio marched for the main doors of the

mansion, aiming to open them in much the same way, when a figure appeared from behind a bush. It was Doug, his fangs dripping red with blood. "Dudes!" he hissed.

"What's *he* doing here?" demanded Resus.

"Do you think it could be Dixon in another shape?" asked Cleo.

"If it is," said Luke, "then who's *that*?" Twinkle appeared from around the corner of the house, smacking his lips. One by one the rest of the Scream Street residents appeared, all with glazed, bloodthirsty expressions on their faces.

"I don't understand," said Cleo to Resus. "Your parents are vampires, but they don't act like this."

"My parents' vampire Energy has been passed down over generations," explained Resus. "This lot have only just been infected – it's new to their systems, which is why they're so thirsty for fresh blood."

"But where are they getting it from?" asked Luke.

"I believe I can answer that!" bellowed a voice from above. Sir Otto and Dixon were leaning out of a first-floor window. "The freezers here are incredibly well-stocked!" The landlord tossed a hunk of beef to the ground, where the vampires pounced upon it, fighting to be the first to feed.

Resus watched in horror. "You're satisfying their bloodlust!" he shouted. "Pushing them deeper beneath the Energy. That's just cruel!"

"Maybe," shrugged Sir Otto, "but they make *such* a better choice of guard dog than my usual breed. You'll have to find your way past them if you want this." He waved *Skipstone's Tales of Scream Street* teasingly.

"You monster!" roared Luke. "You won't be so smug when I let one of them bite me and come after you as a vampire werewolf!"

"Oh, I don't think you'll be doing that," beamed Sir Otto. "You'd still have to slaughter a few of these fools to get inside, and that's hardly likely." With a nasty smile, he tossed a leg of pork to a vampire lurking near the back of the crowd. Mr Watson caught the blood-soaked joint in his fangs and began to tear at the flesh.

"Come on, Dixon," laughed Sir Otto from above. "While they're enjoying the family reunion, let's go and grind some information out of Mr Skipstone!" The window slammed shut as

the landlord and his nephew disappeared.

Luke watched his father bite hungrily into the raw meat. "Dad…"

Cleo rested a hand on his shoulder. "He'll be fine," she said. "We just have to get what we're here for and find a way to cure him."

"I don't see how we're going to get past this lot," said Luke.

"You seem to be forgetting that we've got an army of vampire rats at our disposal!" said Resus. He nodded to Shan, and in response to a harsh *miaow!* from the cat, the front line of rodents dashed forward.

Twinkle flapped his wings and rose into the air before landing on a handful of the rats, crushing them. Doug simply dropped to his knees and fought them on their own level, biting in half any that were slow enough to be caught.

"That wasn't quite what I planned," admitted Resus as a bog monster slurped down a few more of them. The remainder of the rats stayed in their ranks, safe behind Shan.

"That's because you're using them wrongly," said Cleo. "You need to be more creative!" She reached behind Shan and picked up one of the rats, stroking its soft fur. "Give me your fireflies," she said to Resus.

Resus pulled the jar of glowing insects from his cape and handed it to Cleo. The mummy unscrewed the top, dropped the rat inside and closed the jar before shaking it violently.

"It's occurred to me that garlic isn't the only thing vampires are afraid of," she said as a flash of crimson filled the jar. "They hate daylight too!" She opened the container and several huge fireflies shot out, buzzing angrily. Luke and Resus had to shield their eyes from the bright beams of light shining from the Energized insects.

The fireflies zoomed across the grounds of Sneer Hall, sweeping the area like fast-moving searchlights. The vampire residents screamed as the shafts of light flashed across their exposed skin, burning it instantly.

The vampires ran for cover as Cleo removed a slightly dazed rat from the glass jar and placed it gently on the ground. "And that," she said with a smirk, "is how you deal with vampires!"

Resus grinned as he slipped off a false finger-nail and eyed the locks to the mansion's front doors. "Now it's *my* turn to shine!"

 99

*　　*　　*

Luke stepped into the richly carpeted hallway, Resus on one side and Cleo on the other. Shan sat at the mummy's feet, waiting for orders to pass on to the rats.

"Which way?" asked Resus.

"They could be anywhere in here," added Cleo.

"Sneer was using meat from his freezers to feed the vampires," said Luke. "My guess is, they're in the kitchen."

"We don't know where that is," said Resus. "It could take us ages to track them down."

"Not necessarily," replied Luke. He forced an image into his mind: the moment when the Movers had arrived to drag his family from their normal life to the dangers of Scream Street. Anger bubbled at the back of his throat and he pushed it upwards.

The now familiar thin film began to spread across Luke's eyes and he discovered that he could see heat trails in the carpet before him. Two sets of glowing footprints led along the corridor to the left.

"That way," he said.

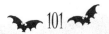

Resus stared into Luke's yellow eyes and laughed. "I think someone is learning to control his transformations!"

Luke allowed the sound of his friend's voice to push the rage away and his eyes returned to normal. "What can I say?" he grinned. "It's a skill!"

He led the group along the corridor until they reached an open doorway to their right. A vast kitchen lay before them. Sir Otto and Dixon were over by one of the sinks. The landlord was holding *Skipstone's Tales of Scream Street* open above the whirring blades of a waste disposal unit while his nephew giggled.

"You have approximately six seconds to tell me where the relics are before your first four chapters are shredded to dust, Skipstone!"

On the cover of the book, Samuel Skipstone's face was a picture of terror. "N-never!" he stammered.

"You know," said Luke, his voice echoing around the steel appliances in the room, "you really ought to treat books with a little more respect!"

Sir Otto spun round and snarled at the sight of

Luke, Resus and Cleo. "Deal with them, Dixon!" he snapped. "And this time, finish the job!"

"Yes, Uncle Otto," Dixon smiled. He grabbed a handful of knives from the nearby worktop and threw them, one after the other, at the trio.

Resus raised a hand, blue sparks crackling around his fingers. He held out his palm and the knives bounced off an invisible shield in front of him. They flew back at Sir Otto's terrified nephew and struck his dusty black coat with deadly accuracy. Within seconds, Dixon was pinned to the kitchen wall.

"Now that," said Luke, "was cool!"

"How did you do it?" exclaimed Cleo.

Resus shrugged. "I've no idea," he admitted. "But I guess that having witch blood inside you isn't so bad after all!" He pointed a sparking blue finger towards the remaining knife. It rose into the air and spun slowly as he turned his hand.

With a flick of the wrist, Resus threw the knife straight at Dixon. The man screamed in terror as the weapon impaled itself in the wall just above his head, severing the ends of a few stray ginger hairs.

"I told you there was a job in the circus waiting for me!" grinned the vampire as he pretended to blow smoke from his fingertips.

Over on the other side of the room, Dixon's skin began to ripple as he changed into a sewer goblin, a creature small enough to escape from his trapped coat.

Cleo smiled. She raced towards the tiny goblin and kicked it hard. With a scream, the creature flew out of the open kitchen window. "That's for pretending to be my dad!" she yelled.

"You idiot, Dixon," barked Sir Otto, snapping *Skipstone's Tales of Scream Street* closed and stuffing it inside his jacket pocket. "But it'll take more than a vampire with a few parlour tricks to get the better of me!" he roared, turning to face the trio.

"What a good idea," said Luke. He nodded to Cleo.

"Shan!" commanded the mummy. The cat sprang to attention beside her. "Introduce Sir Otto to your friends!" Shan leapt up onto one of the ovens and yowled, his fangs glistening in the harsh light of the kitchen.

The polished floor turned black as a river of rats flowed into the room. They scurried up table legs and across worktops, sniffing for fresh meat with which to satisfy their hunger.

Sir Otto Sneer screamed in frustration. "I'll kill you all!" he yelled, backing away from the rats. He grabbed a meat cleaver and gripped its handle tightly.

"Very scary," said Luke. "Now, if you don't mind, I'll become a weapon of my own!" He closed his eyes and pictured his mum, her broken arm wrapped in a cast, crying with fear at the Negative's dinner table. The anger began to flow through his bloodstream once more, but this time Luke allowed it free reign. This time, the rage must consume him.

Chapter Ten
The Kitchen

By the time Luke opened his eyes, he was a fully formed werewolf. He raised his snout to the ceiling and howled. The rats had kept Sir Otto at bay while he transformed, but now, on Shan's command, they parted to allow Luke access to the furious landlord.

With a roar, Sir Otto charged, knocking tables and chairs to one side as he raced for the

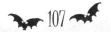

werewolf. Luke leapt gracefully out of the way and the landlord smashed into a fridge, knocking it over and spilling the contents. Within seconds, the rats were all over the food.

Sir Otto turned more quickly than Luke anticipated, swinging the meat cleaver down hard. The werewolf pulled his paw back just in time, the blade of the cleaver slicing off the ends of his long claws as it slammed into the worktop.

"Luke, be careful!" screamed Cleo.

The werewolf lunged for Sir Otto, jaws snapping. The landlord jumped back, catching his foot on a chair leg and crashing to the ground. The meat cleaver skittered away across the tiled floor.

Luke leapt on top of Sir Otto, fangs bared. The man pressed his hands against the wolf's shoulders, pushing back as hard as he could as saliva dripped from the creature's mouth. It hissed as it hit the tip of his burning cigar.

Eyes flashing, Sir Otto thrust his face forward, pressing the glowing end of his cigar into Luke's mouth. The werewolf yelped and fell back before the scorching tobacco burnt his tongue.

Now that Sir Otto was able to move again, he crawled across the kitchen to retrieve the meat cleaver. He stood, eyes scanning the room for the wolf. Luke was perched on one of the ovens, growling deep in his throat.

"This isn't over!" bellowed Sir Otto. He charged again, cleaver held high as he ran across the kitchen. The werewolf dived to one side. Pans clattered to the floor as the landlord ploughed into the cooker, unable to stop himself.

Sir Otto roared in frustration as he tried to turn and attack again. His foot was trapped beneath the heavy oven and he found that he couldn't move.

"Seeing as you're taking a break," Resus teased, "I might do the same myself! Time for a little light reading…" He raised his fingers in the air. Blue light shone from Sir Otto's jacket as *Skipstone's Tales of Scream Street* flew from his pocket, across the kitchen and into the vampire's hand.

"Are you OK, Mr Skipstone?" asked Resus.

The author nodded. "Thank you," he said quietly. Resus slipped the book inside his cloak.

With an angry yell, Sir Otto managed to pull

his foot free and turned to face Luke again. The werewolf leapt across the room as the landlord threw the meat cleaver in his direction.

"It's going to hit him!" Cleo screamed to Resus. "Do something!"

Resus held up a trembling hand, blue sparks fizzing as the magic waited to be released. But what if he pushed the cleaver towards Luke instead of away? "I can't risk it!" he shouted.

Everything seemed to move in slow motion as the cleaver spun towards Luke's exposed stomach. Somehow the wolf twisted out of the way just enough to avoid contact with the glinting blade, crashing to the floor as it embedded itself in the door to a walk-in freezer.

Resus dashed over to Luke. The wolf was dazed but unhurt. "Get the cleaver!" he called to Cleo. "This has to end before Luke gets hurt!"

The mummy raced to the freezer and gripped the handle of the meat cleaver, pulling as hard as she could. It was buried deep in the wood and she was forced to press a foot against the ice-cold door in order to free it.

"Got it!" she shouted as the blade slipped free.

"No!" roared a voice behind her. "*I've* got it!" Sir Otto grabbed Cleo and snatched the cleaver from her hand. "Now," he barked, holding the weapon to the mummy's throat. "Unless you want me to slice your pal here into pieces, I suggest you keep that freak away from me and return my book."

"Don't do it!" yelled Cleo, struggling against the landlord's grip.

Luke leapt to his feet in anger. Resus grabbed

the fur around the werewolf's neck to hold him back.

"Let him go, Resus!" ordered Cleo.

The vampire looked from Cleo to the blade of the meat cleaver, just centimetres from her throat. "I can't…"

Cleo locked her gaze into Resus's. "Trust me," she said. "Let him go."

Resus released his grip on Luke. The werewolf raced towards Sir Otto, claws sliding on the tiled kitchen floor.

"I warned you," yelled the landlord, raising the cleaver above Cleo's head.

"Yes, you did," screeched Cleo, swinging her foot back as far as she could. "But you'll get no warning about *this*!"

The mummy's heel connected with Sir Otto. He squealed, dropping the cleaver and crossing his eyes in pain. Cleo spun round and pulled open the freezer door just as Luke collided with the landlord.

Sir Otto fell, skidding across the icy floor of the freezer and crashing into rack after rack of raw meat, leaving him covered in steaks, chops, ribs and more. Cleo stuck two fingers into her

mouth and whistled. Shan appeared beside her, his eyes sparkling.

Yowling with delight, he led the swarm of rats into the cold room. The creatures began to attack the meat that surrounded Sir Otto. Exhausted, Luke slunk off to the far corner of the kitchen to transform back into human form.

Resus appeared beside Cleo as the landlord disappeared beneath the blanket of rats. "Cleo can call them off before they turn on you," he said. "But only if you tell us where to find the circuit board you took from the filtering machine."

"You'll rot in the Underlands before that happens!" bellowed Sir Otto.

"Very well," said Cleo, beginning to close the door to the freezer room.

"No!" screamed Sir Otto. The raw meat would not last for ever. It wouldn't be long before the rats turned their attention to him. Cleo knew that Shan would stop the rats long before they took a single bite from the terrified landlord, but she wasn't about to tell him that.

"My office!" Sir Otto yelled. "The desk. Bottom drawer. Now get these things off me!"

Resus darted out of the kitchen and ran down the corridor.

Cleo whistled again. Shan hissed at the legion of rats and they scurried out of the freezer. Sir Otto remained on the cold floor, shivering. "You really ought to chill out!" Cleo quipped, swinging the door closed and sliding the bolt into place.

"Will he be all right in there?" asked Luke as the last of his werewolf features faded away. He now stood beside Cleo, human once more.

"Dixon will be back once the coast is clear," she said. "He can let him out. In the meantime, I think he could do with cooling down for a while."

The landlord's face appeared at the small window and he hammered on the door with his fists. "I'll get you!" he bellowed, frost already beginning to form on his eyebrows. "You watch your back, Watson. You haven't seen the last of me!"

Luke reached onto a nearby shelf and grabbed a can of whipped cream. He sprayed it over the surface of the window until Sir Otto was obscured from sight. "I have for now," he said.

Resus appeared in the doorway. "Look what I've found!" he grinned. He was clutching the missing circuit board.

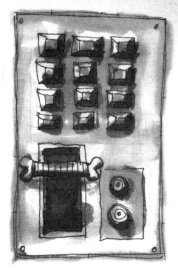

"That just leaves the blockage in the pipe below Sneer Hall," said Cleo.

"Didn't Sir Otto say he'd stuffed the pipe with food?" asked Resus.

"Something like that."

"Then stand back," said the vampire. Pointing his fingers at the waste disposal unit, he let loose a burst of blue flame. It dissolved the spinning blades, exposing the opening to the pipe below.

"Very impressive," grinned Luke.

"There are some things only a new breed of vampire can do!" said Resus.

Cleo clicked her fingers and Shan leapt onto the worktop beside her. "I think your soldiers deserve a feast after a battle like that," she grinned.

The cat yowled to the rats. One after another, the rodents scurried up onto the sink and dived into the pipe.

"Now," said Luke, "we meet them at the other end."

Chapter Eleven
The Filter

Cleo watched as a rat appeared at the end of the pipe, sniffed at the air, then stepped onto her hand. "That's the last of them," she said.

Resus screwed a cap over the pipe and bolted it in place. "OK," he said. "Let's turn this

thing on and see if it works!"

The vampire had slotted the circuit board back into place inside the filtering machine while Luke and Cleo had cleared away the rat's nests and set up some electric lights. The room at the end of the sewer looked brighter already.

"Ready?" asked the vampire.

"Ready!" answered Luke and Cleo together.

Resus pressed a button on the machine's control panel and watched as the gauges rose to normal running capacity. Taking a metal tankard from inside his cloak, Resus opened a tap and filled the container with thick, frothy blood.

"Well?" asked a voice from the corner of the room. "Is it OK?"

"You tell me," said Resus, handing the tankard to his dad. Alston Negative had been shuffling nervously ever since Shan had tracked him down. The older vampire had been collecting used sticking plasters from Scream Street's bins and applying them to his body as temporary blood patches.

Alston took the tankard and drank deeply. "Hey! Slow down, Dad," Resus laughed. "You'll wake up with a bad head tomorrow!"

"Not after this," said Alston. "This is good, pure stuff!"

"He's right," said Cleo as she stroked the rat in her hand. "It seems to have flushed the vampire Energy right out of these little guys' systems."

"Time for the real test, then," said Luke. He turned to his own dad, strapped into a chair beside the machine.

Mr Watson looked up at him with hungry eyes, fangs still jutting through his gums. "Are you sure this will work?"

"I don't see why not," said Luke. "Resus says he's got the tubes connected up to the right parts of the filter."

"I don't mean that," said his dad. "Will it stop me wanting to bite people? Stop me wanting … wanting to drink?"

Luke squeezed his dad's hand. "Once the Energy's filtered out of your blood, you'll be back to fainting at the sight of it, I promise." He nodded to Resus and the vampire knelt beside the chair.

Mr Watson closed his eyes as Resus sank his fake fangs into his arm, quickly strapping a pair of clear rubber tubes over the puncture wounds. Blood began to flow along one of the tubes and into the filtering machine.

"That should be sifting out all the vampire goodness," said Resus as he adjusted the settings slightly. Sticky red liquid appeared in the second tube, running out of the machine and back into Mr Watson's arm.

"How are you feeling?" asked Luke.

"Pretty good," admitted his dad. "I'm starting to think clearly again."

"That's not the only change!" said Cleo, pointing to Mr Watson's mouth. As the trio watched, the fangs pulled slowly back into his upper jaw and his own teeth slid back into place.

"There," said Resus, pulling the tubes free of Mr Watson's arm. "All done!"

Luke's dad sighed with relief. "Will you let me out now?"

"That depends," said Luke, pulling the neck of his top down to expose his throat. "Will you take a bite out of this if I do?"

His dad smiled. "I'd rather have a plate of your mother's lentil bake."

"He's definitely cured!" grinned Luke, undoing the straps that held his father in the chair.

Mr Watson paused on his way out. "Thank you," he said.

"You can thank them after they've topped this up!" called Alston, waving his empty tankard at Resus. The young vampire refilled the container, this time from the blood contaminated with vampire Energy.

"Can't think of a better way to safely dispose of this stuff," he said, handing over the drink.

Alston's fangs clinked against the metal rim of the tankard as he downed the pint in one. "Now that," he said, wiping his lips, "is the good stuff!"

One by one, Resus led the infected residents into the room and connected them to the filtering machine to clean their blood. He had a little trouble finding a working vein in Doug's arm, but after a few hours the only inhabitants of Scream

Street with Energy in their blood were the vampires themselves.

"Here you go, Mr Negative," said Cleo, handing the vampire yet another pint of Energy-loaded blood.

"This'll have to be the last one," Alston groaned, loosening his belt. "I think my fangs are bigger than my belly!" When he eventually left the room, muttering that he needed a lie down, Resus sat in the chair and rolled up his sleeve. "Only one person left to do."

"Are you sure?" asked Luke. "Those witch powers you've got are pretty awesome! They might come in handy."

Resus shook his head. "I'd rather go back to being a pretend vampire," he smiled. "Besides, you need that blood to open a doorway home."

Luke pulled the empty crystal vial from his pocket and slipped one of the clear tubes into it.

"There's just one problem," said Resus. "I can't bite my own arm. You'll have to do it for me."

Luke pulled a face. "OK, I suppose," he said. "Will you lend me your fangs, or would you prefer that I grow my own?"

122

"I think I'd rather keep you in a good mood," said Resus, unclipping his false fangs and handing them over.

Luke bit into his friend's arm, and a few moments later the crystal vial began to fill with blood, blue sparks flashing deep in the swirling liquid.

"My dad got it wrong," said Resus. "*That's* the good stuff!"

"Here you are," said Mrs Watson as she placed a dish on the dining table of 13 Scream Street. The vampires leant closer to take a look.

"It, er, smells lovely!" said Bella. "What is it?"

"My speciality," said Luke's mum. "Lentil bake!"

Resus, Luke and Cleo tried not to laugh as both Mr Watson and Alston Negative screwed up their noses at the same time. "Eat up," said Mrs Watson as she piled the food onto the vampire's plate. "There's plenty more!"

"Oh, good," said Alston, paling a little more than usual and pushing the food around his plate with a fork. The Negatives had agreed to come for dinner to apologize for infecting Luke's dad with Energy. The vampires hadn't expected to be faced with something as terrifying as a meal consisting entirely of vegetables.

"Now," said Mrs Watson, returning from the kitchen with a jug of thick green liquid. "Who wants broccoli sauce?"

Alston clamped a hand over his mouth and dashed out of the room. Resus and Cleo dissolved into fits of laughter.

"Don't worry, Mum," smiled Luke, taking the jug and pouring plenty of the green goo over his own dinner. "I guess it's an acquired taste!"

Cleo nudged his arm and gestured towards the window. Outside in the street, Shan was waiting patiently.

Luke nodded. "We'll be back in a minute," he said as he followed Resus and Cleo to the front door. Shan mewed softly as the trio stepped out into Scream Street. The cat was still the size of a panther and sported vicious fangs.

"I wondered when he'd show up again," said Cleo, tickling the vampire cat under its chin.

"We haven't seen him since Sneer Hall."

"So, what now?" asked Luke. "Will he go back in Resus's cloak, or come to live with you?"

"I don't think he wants to stay in one place any more," said Cleo. "I get the impression he just wants to go where he pleases." Shan mewed and licked her hand as if to agree. "We'll have to do something about those fangs, though."

"You know there's only one way to deal with that, don't you?" said Resus, pulling a heavy crowbar from his cape.

Cleo nodded. "I'd like to do it, if you don't mind." She took the tool, then bent to kiss the cat gently on the nose. "See you again soon."

Luke and Resus looked away as Cleo brought the crowbar down. After a moment, the cat rose into the air, spinning in the midst of another tornado. As the magic subsided, a smaller black cat sat blinking in the moonlight.

"Off you go, then," smiled Cleo. "Start enjoying life number one hundred and forty-two!"

"We should have taken him to Sneer Hall before we did that," said Resus as the kitten padded away. "We could have given Sir Otto one last fright!"

"Nah," Luke grinned. "It could cause havoc with his blood pressure!"

Tommy Donbavand was born and brought up in Liverpool and has worked at numerous careers that have included clown, actor, theatre producer, children's entertainer, drama teacher, storyteller and writer. His non-fiction books for children and their parents, *Boredom Busters* and *Quick Fixes for Bored Kids*, have helped him to become a regular guest on radio stations around the UK and he also writes for a number of magazines, including *Creative Steps* and Scholastic's *Junior Education*.

Tommy sees his new comedy-horror series as what might have resulted had Stephen King been the author of *Scooby Doo*. "Writing *Scream Street* is fangtastic fun," he says. "I just have to be careful not to scare myself too much!" Tommy lives in Northumberland with his family and sees sleep as a waste of good writing time.

You can find out more about Tommy and his books at his website: www.tommydonbavand.com